All Your Own TEETH

For Peter, my heater – A.G.

For Harriet, the armchair adventurer – C.G.
tweet-tweet! tweet-tweet! tweet-tweet!

First published in the United States 2002
by Dial Books for Young Readers
A division of Penguin Putnam Inc.
345 Hudson Street
New York, New York 10014

Published in 2001
by Bloomsbury Publishing Plc
Text copyright © 2001 by Adrienne Geoghegan
Pictures copyright © 2001 by Cathy Gale
All rights reserved
Printed in Hong Kong

1 3 5 7 9 10 8 6 4 2

Library of Congress Cataloging-in-Publication Data
Geoghegan, Adrienne.
All your own teeth/Adrienne Geoghegan; pictures by Cathy Gale.
p. cm.
Summary: Stewart wants to be a real artist and takes the early-morning bus
to the jungle to paint wild animals.
ISBN 0-8037-2655-4
[1. Painting—Fiction. 2. Jungle animals—Fiction. 3. Animals—Fiction.]
I. Gale, Cathy, ill. II. Title.
PZ7.G2927 Al 2002
[E]—dc 21   00-064419

All Your Own TEETH

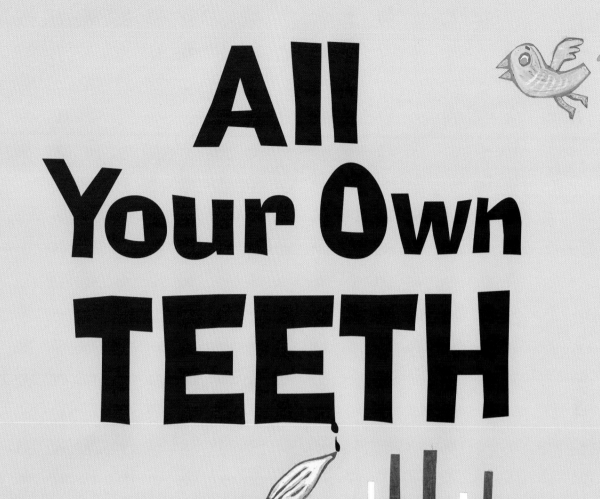

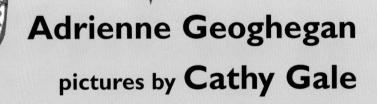

Adrienne Geoghegan

pictures by **Cathy Gale**

Dial Books for Young Readers New York

Stewart was a little boy who
was determined to be an artist.
He painted yellow dogs in clogs
and purple kittens with mittens.
He painted witches and monsters
and big, scary gangsters.

"I am a painter," he said. "**P** is for **Painter**, and **P** is for **Perfect**. I am perfect, but my paintings are not. I need a real model."

He had never painted a real wild animal before. In fact, living in the city, he had never even seen one.

"I'm going to where the wild animals are," said Stewart one day.

BUS
TICKET

He packed his bags and jumped into a taxi. "Hurry to the bus stop," he ordered the taxi driver.

When he arrived in the jungle, he put up his tent in a nice shady spot and unpacked his luggage.

On a big piece of paper he wrote:

WANTED:
Hansum wild animal
to sit still for painting
Must have
all your own teeth
and a nice big smile.

The next morning an elephant saw the sign
and decided to investigate. Stewart was flabbergasted.
He had never seen an elephant before.

"What on earth are you?" he asked.

"I am an elephant,"
she replied. "**E** is for **Elephant**,
and **E** is for **Elegant**."
"Then why," said Stewart, "is that long funnel
thing stuck where your nose should be?"
"It is not a funnel," said the elephant. "It is my trunk."
"Well, an animal with no nose is of no use to me," said
Stewart. "I am looking for a perfect model."

The elephant felt terribly insulted.
She went off to the watering hole
to recover with a nice cool drink of water.

The following day a cheetah spotted
the sign and wandered over to the tent.
Stewart was shocked.
He had never seen a cheetah before.

"And just who do you think you are?" asked Stewart.
"I am a cheetah," he replied.
"**C** is for **Cheetah,** and **C** is for **Charming**."

"Charming?" laughed Stewart.
"Well, I certainly won't be charmed if I catch those spots!"
"They are not contagious," replied the cheetah.
"They are what make me a cheetah."

"Well, a big spotty beast
is of no use to me,"
said Stewart. "I am looking
for a perfect
model."

The cheetah was absolutely disgusted.
He joined the insulted elephant
at the watering hole and checked
his complexion.

Early the next morning a giraffe decided to try her luck. She lingered by the tent for a while. Stewart came outside and saw four long legs.

He looked UP . . .

and up . . . and up.

"Good grief!"
He had never seen
a giraffe before.

"WHAT ARE YOU UP THERE?" he shouted.
"I am a giraffe," she replied
as she bent down to look at him.
"**G** is for **Giraffe**, and **G** is for **Graceful**."
"Ha ha ha!" laughed Stewart.
"With a neck like that, you are far from graceful!"
"It is there for a very good reason," said the giraffe.
"Well, I am here for a very good reason," said Stewart,
"and I certainly don't want to paint a lanky-necked
thing like you. I am looking for a perfect model."

The giraffe was awfully embarrassed.

She joined the insulted elephant and the disgusted cheetah by the watering hole and tried to compose herself.

Stewart frowned at his large blank piece of paper.
He was fed up with waiting for a wild animal
and was almost tempted to paint
another tree.

Then he heard a heavy thud, thud, thud, and all his paintbrushes rattled in their jars. He got up and found a huge muddy animal outside. He had never seen a hippopotamus before.

"And what, may I ask, are you?" said Stewart.

"I am a hippopotamus," he replied.

"**H** is for **Hippopotamus**, and **H** is for **Handsome**."

"How ridiculous!" said Stewart.

"You are far too dirty to be handsome."

"The mud keeps me cool," said the hippopotamus.

"Well, you'd look like a big splotch of chocolate pudding
on my nice clean paper. I am looking for a perfect model!"

So the hippo went to join the insulted elephant,
the disgusted cheetah, and the embarrassed giraffe.
He sank down very sadly into the watering hole
until all you could see were his eyes and his nostrils.

Stewart decided enough was enough.
"That's it," he said. "I'm sick of this place
and all these ugly animals."
As he was packing to leave,
an enormous crocodile came by.
He stopped to read Stewart's sign:

WANTED:
Hansum wild animal
to sit still for painting
Must have
all your own teeth
and a nice big smile.

Stewart had never seen a crocodile before.
"And before you ask who I am," the animal said, grinning,
"I am a crocodile, and I have all my own teeth
and a nice BIG perfect smile."
"Sh…sh…shuuure, Mr. Crocodile," said Stewart,
unpacking his stuff. "How would you like me to paint you?"
"With all my friends, of course!" said the crocodile
with an engaging smile.

And along came
the **Elegant Elephant**,
the **Charming Cheetah**,
the **Handsome Hippopotamus**,
and the **Graceful Giraffe**.

"SSSSmmmile," said Stewart,
trembling behind his big sheet of paper.
"A little wider please, Mr. Crocodile.
Let's see those perfect white teeth of yours—"

SNAP!

"Yum, Yum, Yum!"

The crocodile grinned.

"**P** is for **Painter**, and **P** is for **Picnic**." He burped. "How perfect."